To Mom and Dad

Published by Feiwel & Friends
Feiwel & Friends is an imprint of Macmillan Publishing Group, LLC
Paperback published by Square Fish, an imprint of Macmillan Publishing Group, LLC
120 Broadway, New York, NY 10271
mackids.com
Copyright © 2016 by Nilah Magruder.
All rights reserved.

Printed and bound in Mexico by Procesos y Acabados en Artes Gráficas S.A. de C.V.
Square Fish and the Square Fish logo are trademarks of Macmillan and
are used by Feiwel & Friends under license from Macmillan.

Our books may be purchased in bulk for promotional, educational, or business use.
Please contact your local bookseller or the Macmillan Corporate and Premium Sales Department
at (800) 221-7945 ext. 5442 or by email at MacmillanSpecialMarkets@macmillan.com.

Library of Congress Cataloging-in-Publication Data
Names: Magruder, Nilah, author.
Title: How to find a fox / Nilah Magruder.
Description: First Edition. | New York : Feiwel and Friends, 2016.
Identifiers: LCCN 2015042041 | ISBN 9781250086563 (hardback)
Subjects: | CYAC: Foxes—Fiction. | BISAC: JUVENILE FICTION / Animals / Foxes. | JUVENILE FICTION /
Social Issues / Self-Esteem & Self-Reliance | JUVENILE FICTION / Action & Adventure / General.
Classification: LCC PZ7.1.M316 Ho 2016 | DDC [E]—dc23
LC record available at http://lccn.loc.gov/2015042041

Originally published in the United States by Feiwel & Friends
First Square Fish edition, 2022
Square Fish logo designed by Filomena Tuosto

ISBN: 978-1-250-08656-3 (hardcover)
5 7 9 10 8 6 4

ISBN: 978-1-250-84656-3 (paperback)
3 5 7 9 10 8 6 4 2

HOW TO FIND A FOX

Nilah Magruder

SQUARE FISH   Feiwel and Friends   New York

How to find a fox:

Find a fox hole.

Any fox hole
will do.

The best foxes are at home
when you visit.

Take out your fox bait.

Place it somewhere easy to spot.

Hide. Then wait very quietly.

Wait a little longer.

Maybe you should try
a different approach.

Tread slowly over the ground.
Foxes have keen hearing.

You don't want to
startle them.

Be sure to look for
fox tracks.

They're like dog tracks,
but sneakier.

Take a picture of a family of raccoons.

They have bushy tails kind of like foxes.

Put out more bait.

Wait longer this time.

Oh no! You waited too long.

Lying around won't bring foxes to you. Keep looking.

Stalk through the grass.
Make fox calls.

Search by the stream. Make more fox calls.

Roll down a hill.
It won't help you find
a fox, but it's fun.

Maybe you need a change of perspective.

Climb a tree.

Slowly . . .

Carefully . . .

There he is!

Run, run!

You've got to be quick.

Don't lose him!

You lost him.

Kick a rock.

No, wait.
Not that one.

Kick a
smaller rock.

Lie down on your back because it's hopeless.

Perhaps this was the wrong day to find foxes.

Maybe you should just give up.

You want to go home,

but you're too tired.

What do you do now?

Take deep breaths.

Close your eyes.

Take a walk in your mind.

Now's not the time to give up.

What you're looking for is closer than you think.

You've got a feeling that it's staring you right in the face.....

Some days, a fox doesn't want to be found.

Some days, he wants to find YOU!

Congratulations! You are a master at finding foxes!